Mapping the Heart: The Doctor's Odyssey

Dr Andrew C S Koh

Published by Dr Andrew C S Koh, 2024.

COPYRIGHT

Table of Contents

Dedicated to my beloved wife Wai Yin, my sons, daughters-in-laws, grandsons, granddaughters, and to the glory of God.

Quiet prayer from the eyes of patients

The doctor's journey is revealed.

Inspire, not just repair.

Light the world up with holy fire

Now, words are replacing the blade's edge.

His pen is a solemn promise of a healer.

His map grows through books and stories.

To lead new hearts to distant lands.

The journey is the art of this life.

Maps are not only for the flesh,

But also for the heart..

FOREWORD

Dr. Robert Carter stressed the importance of appreciating his journey, highlighting the value of his impact on others, the differences he made, and the lessons learned along the way.

"Mapping the Heart: The Doctor's Odyssey" goes beyond fiction; it highlights human resilience, faith, and the importance of service. Dr. Carter's journey highlights the importance of compassion, integrity, and purpose in medicine, emphasizing the crucial role of dedicated service in today's society.

This extraordinary narrative chronicles a transformative journey from modest rural beginnings to esteemed universities and the demanding realm of cardiology. It clearly shows the protagonist's struggles and successes as he faces challenges, embraces his purpose, and uses his abilities to heal physical and emotional pain.

Though fictional, this narrative resonates with authenticity by drawing upon timeless themes of struggle, perseverance and redemption. Dr. Carter's journey teaches us that true satisfaction comes from serving others and staying true to our values, not just achieving milestones.

This book offers an insightful look at living a meaningful life, appealing to medical professionals, inspiration seekers, and anyone interested in captivating stories.

May these pages inspire you to face your own journey with courage and conviction, just like Dr. Carter. His story reminds us that every heart, no matter how broken or burdened, can find meaning and rhythm again.

Welcome to Mapping the Heart: The Doctor's Odyssey
Pastor Peter Ku Kit Wan

2nd December 2024

PREFACE

"Mapping the Heart: The Doctor's Odyssey" tells the fictional story of Dr. Robert Carter, who faces personal and professional challenges while experiencing significant spiritual growth.

This book is a work of fiction, created solely from imagination. Any resemblance to real people or events in this story is purely coincidental. All characters, places, and events are fictional and intended for storytelling purposes.

"Mapping the Heart" delves into timeless themes of resilience, purpose, and faith through Dr. Carter's inspiring journey. This narrative encourages readers to think about their lives and reflect on important questions, such as what motivates us to overcome challenges. How can we channel our unique talents and gifts for the benefit of others? And where do we find meaning amidst life's obstacles?

This book is designed not just for medical professionals, but for anyone seeking inspiration. It celebrates human resilience and shows how empathy and integrity can positively impact our world.

May this story touch your heart and inspire you to navigate your own path with bravery and determination.

Dr. Andrew C S Koh,

2nd December 2024

THE STORY BEHIND MAPPING THE HEART

Excerpt

"Mapping the Heart: The Doctor's Odyssey" intertwines the personal journey of Dr. Robert Carter, a cardiologist, with themes of resilience, compassion, and healing. The novel emphasizes the significance of emotional and spiritual well-being in medicine. It serves as a tribute to doctors and patients, encouraging deeper connections and understanding in the healing process.

The Inspiration Behind the Book

"Mapping the Heart: The Doctor's Odyssey" draws inspiration from my journey as a physician. As a former cardiologist, I experienced many moments of profound human connection, marked by both triumph and adversity. This fictional odyssey is a reflection of those impactful encounters, emphasizing the deep-rooted essence of healing.

This novel explores themes of resilience, compassion, and purpose through the journey of a healer. Through vivid storytelling, the narrative explores the intricate tapestry of life that binds patients and doctors together. Each chapter unfolds a new lesson that underscores the transformative power of empathy in the practice of medicine.

The Journey of Dr. Robert Carter

Dr. Robert Carter's story is about a dedicated cardiologist facing challenges in his job, spiritual struggles, and personal difficulties. Throughout his journey, we witness a profound exploration of faith and the resilience of the human spirit. Dr. Carter is at a crossroads in his career, questioning his beliefs and the influence he has on his patients. He learns that healing involves not just the physical, but also emotional and spiritual aspects that are essential to life.

Robert's experiences shed light on the connection between science and faith, highlighting significant personal moments that shape his healing career. Robert's story spans from saving lives in a cath lab to contemplative times at theology college. It captures the journey of a doctor not just physically, but also spiritually.

Themes Explored

This book explores important questions about life. It focuses on key themes like resilience and compassion. These are two indispensable qualities for achieving success both personally and professionally. It delves into the interplay of medicine and morality, urging readers to think about their own beliefs and biases. Ultimately, it is a journey of self-discovery, encouraging a holistic approach to healing that transcends traditional boundaries.

Discovering purpose in your career or vocation should be your foremost aim. By embracing this journey, one can unlock a deeper understanding of what it truly means to heal. Robert explores the intersection of medicine and spirituality, encouraging readers to redefine success beyond just achievements. This story delves into the connection between medicine and spirituality. It follows a physician who goes beyond physical healing. The physician works to restore lives and nurture souls.

A Tribute for Doctors and Patients

"Mapping the Heart" is my sincere homage to the devoted doctors. They work tirelessly to heal. It also honors the patients who show both the fragility and strength of the human spirit. Each consultation, procedure, and conversation between doctor and patient shows a shared experience that deserves recognition and appreciation. In this tapestry of care, we witness the profound impact that empathy and compassion can have in the healing process. It serves as a reminder that beyond medical skill, human connection is key. It ultimately paves the way for true recovery.

An Invitation to Readers

This book transcends mere storytelling; it delves deeply into every facet of heart health—physical, mental, and spiritual. It also reflects my personal journey, inviting readers to uncover their own truths within its pages. As we embark on this exploration together, I encourage each of you to embrace your individual experiences and insights. Together, we can foster a greater understanding of heart health in all its dimensions.

"Mapping the Heart, The Doctor's Odyssey" is an inspiring journey of self-discovery for everyone, regardless of profession or faith. Through shared stories and practical wisdom, we will illuminate the pathways to a healthier heart and spirit. This book is both a guide and a companion for anyone looking to enhance their life and relationships.

CHAPTER 1

GROWING UP IN MAPLE GROVE: A DREAM OF MEDICINE

Excerpt

Robert Carter grows up in Maple Grove, inspired by his compassionate parents. Despite financial struggles, his curiosity and love for reading lead him to dream of becoming a doctor. Robert cultivates his aspirations through community acts of kindness. He receives unwavering family support. He envisions a future where he can help others and make a difference.

A Quiet Beginning in Maple Grove

As the sun rose and light filled his small home on Elm Street, Robert Carter's life began. It was within this picturesque backdrop that his story truly unfolded. Robert spent his childhood exploring the wonders of Maple Grove, surrounded by rustling leaves and chirping birds. Each day brought new adventures, shaping his dreams and igniting his curiosity about the world beyond his quiet town. He often wandered to the forest's edge. There, the trees seemed to whisper secrets of distant lands and untold stories. These moments of solitude fueled his imagination, planting the seeds of aspirations that would one day blossom into something extraordinary.

Robert Carter was the middle child of George and Margaret, who had three children. His father was a schoolteacher and his mother a nurse. They influenced his upbringing with stories of perseverance, lessons in compassion, and occasional chaos. Robert dealt with middle-child syndrome by finding comfort in books that took him beyond his small town. This love of story illuminated his path. It guided him toward a future crafted by words. His future is also woven with dreams.

A Curious and Different Child

Robert was different from most children his age. While other kids played outside, Robert preferred reading his father's encyclopedia or sketching the anatomy of nearby amphibians. His innate curiosity often led him to explore the world around him in ways others couldn't understand. This unique perspective formed the basis of his creative imagination. It allowed him to see beauty and complexity in the simplest of things.

Rob was often found with his nose in a book, prompting James, his older brother, to tease him about it.

"Why don't you join us for a game instead of staring at those boring pages?" James chuckled. Robert simply smiled. He knew that in those pages lay adventures greater than any game would offer. They had no idea that Robert's insatiable thirst for knowledge would lead him to make astounding discoveries.

Robert offered as his reasoning: "Because one day, I will need this knowledge," with hazel eyes beaming with determination.

James rolled his eyes. Yet, he couldn't help but admire Robert's passion. It seemed to glow brighter with every turn of a page. As the years went by, that same determination began to shape Robert's path in ways they would never have imagined.

Margaret swiftly discerned Robert's inquisitiveness. To appease it, Margaret brought home old medical charts and anatomy posters from the clinic where she worked. Robert would then spend hours poring over these charts, piecing together his body like a puzzle. His fascination grew into a strong wish to understand the human body's complexities. He dreamed of one day becoming a doctor. Those late nights spent in a world of diagrams and labels solidified his ambition. They fueled his resolve to pursue a future in medicine.

A Transformational Moment

Life in Maple Grove wasn't without its challenges. Robert Carter's family wasn't wealthy. Every penny had to stretch far and wide. Despite their financial struggles, Robert's determination never wavered, as he found ways to excel in school and earn scholarships. His relentless pursuit of knowledge became a beacon of hope for his family. It encouraged them to believe that a better future was within reach. Robert supported his parents' household needs. He extended kindness toward his neighbors. Robert would often help repair leaky roofs or deliver soup. It was on one such visit where Robert saw an act that would transform his future forever.

Mrs. Carter, an elderly widow living down the street, was struggling to carry her groceries inside. Without a moment's hesitation, Margaret rushed to her side. As Margaret assisted her, Robert learned about the importance of community. He also discovered the strength found in kindness. Holloway, an elderly woman with sunken cheeks and shaking hands, thanked Margaret.

She took a sip from her warm broth bowl. "You have saved my life again!"

Margaret extended a gentle hand to comfort the woman.

With a warm smile, she replied, "It's just a small gesture, really."

The grateful look in Holloway's eyes filled Margaret with a sense of purpose she had never experienced before.

"We're all here to support each other," she replied, adding, "and you needn't feel afraid. Let us work together to support one another."

Robert watched as his young mind absorbed the weight of his mother's words, taking them all in. That night, Robert lay awake in his small bed staring at the ceiling. For the first time, he imagined life outside Maple Grove. He considered the possibility that one day he will help people when they needed assistance most. The thought filled him with excitement and determination, a flicker of hope igniting within. As he closed his eyes, he envisioned a future. He thought of making a difference just like his mother had done for Holloway.

A Dream Is Born

Robert started to cultivate his aspirations at a remarkably tender age. He asked his father for books on science and spent hours shadowing his mother at her clinic. He soaked up every piece of knowledge, driven by a longing to understand the intricacies of healing. Each moment spent learning brought him closer to his dream, fueling his wish to serve those in need.

By 12, Robert announced aloud his dream: "I want to become a doctor!"

Lily laughed with delight as her brother James laughed, while George nodded his approval with pride. Margaret shed tears nonetheless. She saw in Robert the same passion which once drove her. She vowed to nurture it no matter the cost. She promised herself that she would support Robert's ambitions, even if it meant sacrificing her own desires. With unwavering resolve, she began to gather resources and connect with mentors who would guide him on his path.

This feisty youngster from Maple Grove became someone extraordinary. As the years passed, Robert immersed himself in his studies, fueled by the unwavering support of his family. Margaret often reminded him of their journey together, igniting a shared passion that would forever shape their destinies. As they navigated the challenges ahead, Margaret found herself inspired by Robert's dedication and resilience. Together, they dream of his success. They also imagine a future where they would uplift others and create a legacy of hope and ambition.

CHAPTER 2

BREAKING THE CYCLE OF POVERTY THROUGH EDUCATION

Excerpt

In Maple Grove, poverty and despair consumed the community due to failed crops and limited healthcare. Robert Carter recognized the need for change and advocated for education and sustainable farming. He organized workshops, enhancing health outcomes and fostering resilience. His vision of a future clinic embodies healing and education, planting seeds of hope.

Maple Grove

Maple Grove was an idyllic village, yet wracked with hardship. Behind its picturesque beauty lay an unsettling reality. The crops had failed for the past two seasons, leaving families struggling to make ends meet. As whispers of despair echoed through the narrow roads, the once-vibrant community began to fracture under the weight of uncertainty. One beset by poverty, ignorance, and superstition. These experiences were burdensome but also enriching. They allowed Robert Carter to recognize the urgent need for change. Determined to break the cycle of despair, he set out to educate the community about sustainable farming practices. With each passing day, he cultivated the land. He also nurtured hope among the people who had long felt abandoned.

Witnessing the Suffering

The Carters lived in a simple house at the town's edge, with fields stretching out toward the horizon. Although farming provided their livelihood, many struggled to make ends meet when crops failed or illnesses took their toll. These contributed to an ever-increasing cycle of poverty that often went unrecognized and untreated. Robert knew that breaking this cycle required a multi-faceted approach. He began organizing workshops to teach families about nutrition and healthcare. He also included sustainable cultivation techniques in these teachings. Slowly but surely, the community started to embrace these teachings, igniting a newfound sense of resilience and purpose.

Robert felt helpless whenever he saw one of his neighbors suffering from preventable diseases. He was determined to make a change. He sought partnerships with local healthcare providers. His goal was to bring preventive care and education directly to the community. With each passing week, the workshops improved health outcomes. They also fostered a spirit of collaboration and hope among the families. Coughing, festering wounds, or high fever would claim lives. This happened due to lack of access to healthcare. It also occurred because people relied on outdated beliefs instead of seeking professional medical help.

Robert vividly remembered the day Mr. Jenkins, a farmer down the road, died. Rather than seeking medical help for his worsening fever, Mr. Jenkins insisted upon burning sage and saying prayers as a cure. This memory remains fresh in Robert's mind. He and his mother paid their respects. The Jenkins family were deeply upset at losing him. Robert stood alongside her at his memorial service. Their grief had left an indelible mark upon him. The sun began to set, casting a soft glow over the somber gathering. Robert felt a mix of sorrow and empathy for the family he had known all his life. He understood that this loss would greatly affect the community. It highlighted the need for connection and support in times of heartbreak.

Robert was confused. He didn't understand why they hadn't brought him in for treatment at the clinic. Later, he asked his mother why this hadn't happened sooner. His mother looked at him with tear-filled eyes, struggling to find the right words to explain. She finally whispered that the family's pride often overshadowed their need for help. It was a reminder that sometimes even the strongest among them needed to lean on others.

Margaret sighed, her expression showing fatigue. She had been carrying the weight of their struggles for too long. She tried to keep the family together in the face of adversity. Robert would see the toll it had taken on her. He decided to step up. He wanted to support her in any way possible.

"Rob, people often fear what they don't understand, and sometimes they simply lack the resources."

The Power of Education

Robert was profoundly moved by these moments. They opened his eyes to the incredible power and potential benefits of education. He also realized its devastating costs in absence. He knew that knowledge would be the key to unlocking a brighter future for his family. It would also help the surrounding community. With renewed determination, Robert decided to advocate for more accessible educational resources. He believed that empowering others would ultimately strengthen their ties. This approach would also foster resilience. While others accepted life as it was, Robert dreamed of more. He desired to understand more of human anatomy so he would bring about healing instead of ignorance.

His father often found him reading late into the night. George would often tell him that there are no shortcuts to knowledge. He encouraged Rob to continue learning until he found what he needed. With each page he turned, Robert felt a spark of hope. It ignited within him. This feeling fueled his ambition to make a difference. He resolved to blend his passion for learning with action. He dreamed of a community where education was a bridge, not a barrier.

"Keep at it," George would suggest with pride in his voice. "Keep exploring, and you may just discover where your answers lie!"

Robert persevered. His peers laughed at his endless questions. They made fun of his fascination with science. He disregarded their remarks with ease. Each piece of knowledge and inspiration gleaned from his mother's stories and experiences in her clinic fueled his determination. He dreamed of opening his own clinic. It would be a place that fostered learning and healing for those who were often overlooked. With every story shared, Robert inched closer to that dream. Every lesson learned prepared him to transform his aspirations into reality.

The Drive to Escape Poverty

Robert Carter had seen first-hand how hard his parents worked to supply for their family despite significant sacrifice. Their determined efforts to improve their lives motivated Robert. He was inspired to break the cycle of poverty that had burdened them for generations. He would strive for his own success. He would also uplift those around him. He created a legacy of hope and opportunity.

He began to change for himself. His motivation extended to his family and the community of Maple Grove as well. Becoming a doctor wasn't simply his dream. It represented freedom from poverty while offering hope to those around him. Each late-night study session brought him closer to understanding the complexities of medicine. Understanding these complexities gave him a sense of purpose. Robert envisioned his future clinic not just as a medical facility. He saw it as a hub for education and empowerment. It would be a place where knowledge was shared. Lives were transformed there.

"Rob, when the time comes don't forget where you came from!" His father advised, him, patting him on the back after another long day working the fields.

Robert nodded, knowing that the roots of his journey were anchored deeply in the values his parents instilled in him. With every step ahead, he promised to carry their sacrifice with him. This would inspire the compassion he would offer to his future patients.

A Seed Planted

Robert saw in Maple Grove's struggles a constant reminder of why he wanted to work for change. Replacing fear with understanding, suffering with healing, and poverty with opportunity. He envisioned a future where every child had access to the education they deserved, fostering a generation of change-makers. As he continued to cultivate his knowledge, Robert knew he was planting seeds of hope. These seeds would one day blossom into something extraordinary for his community. Each hardship, story of loss and small victory strengthened Robert's resolve and inspired his dedication.

Robert was still young when he realized his calling. He understood that making a true impact required combining his ambitions with the heart of the community. He needed to listen to their needs and respond with sensitivity. With that clarity, Robert began to devise a plan for his future clinic. It would not only treat ailments but also educate families on health and wellness. This would guarantee the strength of Maple Grove for generations to come.

He did not realize that his seeds of ambition would one day bear fruit in amazing ways. These seeds were planted in the challenging soil of adversity. Robert lay awake at night, sketching out ideas for his clinic on the back of old receipts. He felt a growing sense of purpose. Each vision became a blueprint for change, igniting a fire within him that promised to fuel his journey ahead. He spent countless hours refining his ideas, fueled by the belief that education and healing would coexist in harmony. With every line drawn, Robert was not just mapping out a clinic. He was charting a course towards hope for a community yearning for brighter days.

CHAPTER 3

HOW A SCHOLARSHIP CHANGED ROBERT'S LIFE

Excerpt

Robert Carter was a dedicated student from Maple Grove High. He transformed his aspirations into reality through hard work. He achieved a prestigious scholarship to St. Anne's University. He relentlessly pursued knowledge. His passion for science inspired peers and the community. Ultimately, this propelled him toward a fulfilling journey in medical school to serve others.

A Student With a Purpose

Robert Carter stood out at Maple Grove High, not because of his clothes or social status, which were both ordinary. It was his insatiable curiosity and relentless drive that distinguished him from his peers. He sought knowledge in every corner of his life, asking questions that often left others pondering in silence. His determination pushed him to take on challenges that most students avoid, inspiring his classmates.

While most would avoid math or chemistry-related challenges, Robert welcomed them as opportunities. He participated in every science fair and math competition, often mentoring his fellow students along the way. His enthusiasm was infectious, gradually transforming the perception of these subjects into something exciting rather than daunting. Books became his refuge, knowledge his weapon against life's difficulties.

Robert was quickly recognized by his teachers. Mrs. Thompson, his biology instructor, often commented on Robert's potential.

She would tell him, "Robert, you have an extraordinary gift. "Don't let this small town hold you back."

With each passing day, he became more determined to seize every opportunity that came his way.

Her words motivated him to study late into the night by the dim kerosene lamp. He immersed himself in textbooks and research papers, eager to expand his understanding of the world beyond his small town. As the stars twinkled outside, he dreamed of the future and the impact he would make through science.

Balancing Work and Study

Harmonizing Work and Study Life wasn't easy for Robert even though he excelled academically. His family depended on him for help with chores and odd jobs. This often left him tired. Yet, he remained determined to support them. He devised a strict schedule, allocating time for studies while ensuring he fulfilled his responsibilities at home. Despite the exhaustion, he felt a deep sense of purpose. He knew that both his education and family were worth the sacrifices he made.

"I can't give up now," he often reminded himself.

Every challenge he faced only fueled his ambition further. With unwavering resolve, he continued to push the boundaries of his knowledge, convinced that a brighter tomorrow awaited him. "There's too much at stake."

Robert's sacrifices paid off. By his final year of high school, Robert was consistently at the top of his class. This brought pride to both himself and his family, while garnering significant notice from local community members. They began to see him as a beacon of hope for the younger generation. His achievements inspired them to pursue their dreams with the same fervor. As graduation approached, Robert felt an exhilarating mix of excitement and anxiety about the next chapter of his life.

A Life-Changing Opportunity

One day, Robert was summoned by the school principal into his office. As he walked in, the principal smiled. He gestured for Robert to take a seat. He revealed that a prestigious scholarship had become available to a select few students. This would be the chance of a lifetime. It opens doors to renowned universities. It also provides the opportunity to study in an environment that nurtured innovation and creativity. Mr. Whitman continued, "I submitted your name."

Robert was overjoyed. A scholarship? Attending university had long seemed out of reach, yet now it was within his reach. His heart raced with possibilities. He imagined himself standing on a campus bustling with ideas and dreams. Robert was determined not to waste this opportunity. He promised himself to put forth every ounce of effort needed. This would secure his place there!

Margaret and George Carter spent months of preparation and hopeful anticipation, waiting anxiously for news of acceptance letters. Finally, the day arrived when the letters were sent out, and the air was thick with excitement and tension. As Robert tore open the envelope, his eyes widened in disbelief. He had been accepted. Relief washed over him. He knew that all his hard work had truly paid off. Their emotions overflew any effort at restraint.

"You've accomplished it," George exclaimed with tears welling in his eyes.

Margaret embraced Robert tightly, pride radiating from her as she whispered, "You've made us so proud."

Dreams he'd imagined for years were now becoming a reality. He was ready to embrace the future with open arms.

His journey was just beginning. "You have opened a door we never believed was possible."

A Prestigious Beginning

Receiving a scholarship wasn't just any pass to study medicine at St. Anne's University, one of the country's premier educational facilities. It was a golden ticket to a world of knowledge. It provided opportunity and potential. He would cultivate his passion for science and make a tangible difference. As Robert took his first steps onto the sprawling campus, he felt an electric sense of possibility. This surge of energy ignited his determination to leave a lasting mark.

Robert was both anxious and excited as he prepared to leave Maple Grove for the first time. Family and friends gathered outside his train car to give their final farewells. Their expressions ranged from prideful smiles to sorrowful ones. He felt a mix of emotions as he glanced back. The faces of his loved ones were forever etched in his memory. He carried their support and his fervent aspirations. With determination, he stepped ahead into the bright unknown. He was ready to transform his dreams into reality.

"Remember where you came from," his mother reminded him as she pressed a handwritten letter into his palm. *"Never stop working to make a difference,"* she added.

He clutched the letter tightly, its contents a reminder of his roots and the love that propelled him ahead. As the train pulled away, Robert vowed to honor that promise. He fueled his journey with determination. He had a wish to uplift those who had always believed in him.

As the train pulled away, Robert turned back toward his hometown to pledge its memory with him wherever life led. He could already envision the challenges and triumphs that awaited him ahead. Each step would mold him into the person he aspired to be. Robert felt gratitude and ambition in his heart. He was ready to embrace the adventure. He knew that every lesson learned at St. Anne's would bring him closer to his goals.

A New Chapter Begins

At St. Anne's, Robert quickly adjusted to the rigorous demands of medical school. Surrounded by brilliant peers and stimulating mentors, he felt both challenged and exhilarated. This new chapter marked his journey toward becoming the physician he always dreamed of being. He immersed himself in lectures, absorbing every piece of information with the same tenacity that propelled him through high school. Late nights in the library became a new norm. The thrill of learning in such an inspiring environment outweighed the fatigue.

Every lecture, lab session, and sleepless night was one step closer to fulfilling his mission. His mission was to heal, serve, and give back to the community that had helped form him. He formed friendships with fellow students who shared his passion. They created a supportive network. This network fueled their ambitions further.

Together, they faced the challenges of coursework and examinations. They celebrated each other's achievements. They reminded one another of the dreams that brought them to St Anne's in the first place. They spent long hours studying together. They shared meals full of laughter. They strengthened each other's resolve. They knew their hard work was paving the way for a future. They would truly make a difference in the world.

CHAPTER 4

FROM MEDICAL STUDENT TO DOCTOR

Excerpt

Robert Carter's journey from student to physician at St. Anne's University is marked by excitement and intense study. Embracing his calling amid overwhelming challenges, he bonds with peers, navigates rigorous coursework, and ultimately earns his MBBS degree. Now as Dr. Robert Carter, he is ready to make a meaningful impact in healthcare.

A New World of Learning

Stepping onto the grand halls of St. Anne's University was like walking into another world for Robert Carter. The impressive buildings, bustling with students from different backgrounds, contrasted sharply with his modest life in Maple Grove. As he looked at the crowd, he felt both excited and nervous about his dream of becoming a doctor. Every corner seemed to whisper promises of knowledge and opportunity, urging him to embrace this new chapter.

Robert experienced an exciting and memorable first week. Robert engaged in orientation sessions and met his professors. He experienced the anatomy dissection room firsthand. He was brimming with anticipation. He found himself captivated by the intricate details of the human body, each revelation deepening his wish to learn more. Late nights spent studying with new friends fueled his passion, solidifying his commitment to the journey ahead.

"Welcome to anatomy class!" announced Dr. Williams, greeting students in her department for their first class. She continued, "Today you start learning about its mysteries. Let's explore the complexities of the human body, beginning with the skeleton."

The lecture began. Robert felt a surge of excitement. He knew this was the start of a transformative adventure in his medical career.

Robert was quickly drawn in by anatomy after his first lecture and dissection. Holding a scalpel for the first time, Robert felt a heavy weight of responsibility.

"This is where it all begins," he thought to himself while keeping his hands steady.

The air was thick with focus as he made his first incision. A wave of both fear and excitement washed over him. With each careful cut, he realized he was not just learning about bones and muscles. He was embracing the very essence of life itself.

Life on Campus

Campus life was full of life and activity. Students rushed from one lecture to the next, laughter echoing down the hallways as friendships blossomed over shared experiences. Late-night study sessions in cozy libraries became a norm, fueling both their academic pursuits and their growing sense of community. Robert quickly connected with an intimate circle of medical students. Together, they spent countless hours in the library. They shared meals at the cafeteria and supported each other through moments of self-doubt.

There were breaks, sports days, and cultural festivals. There were also late-night discussions under the campus stars. The demanding curriculum left little time for leisure activities. Yet, they found ways to balance their workload with bursts of joy, often organizing impromptu study breaks to recharge. These moments of laughter and support not only strengthened their friendships. They also reinforced their determination to succeed in their challenging program.

"Medicine is more than a career; it's a calling." This statement would come to Robert's mind whenever his workload seemed daunting. He understood that each challenge was a stepping stone. It reminded him of the lives he hoped to impact in the future. As the semester progressed, Robert's passion for medicine deepened, intertwining with friendships that became just as vital to his journey.

Struggles of a Medical Student

Robert was surprised at the intensity and volume of material to cover in medical school over five years. Anatomy, biochemistry, physiology, pharmacology, parasitology, pathology, and clinical rotations were just the tip of the iceberg. Each discipline demanded not only memorization but also a deep understanding of intricate connections within the body. The workload was overwhelming at times. Yet, Robert found solace in the study groups. These groups pushed them all to persevere and grow together.

Anatomy class was his favorite topic. The dissection lab offered him hands-on understanding of human anatomy. He often stayed behind late studying cadavers and charts to master every detail. The quiet hum of the lab let him connect deeply with the material. Each session became a personal exploration of the human form. With each passing day, Robert's confidence grew. This boosted his wish to uncover even more about the complexities of human health. He was keen on learning the art of healing.

His journey included many obstacles. There were times when exhaustion reduced him to tears. Doubts also crept into his mind about whether he could keep going ahead. But his purpose, inspired by witnessing suffering in Maple Grove, kept him pushing onward. The memories of those he wished to help became a driving force, reminding him that every sacrifice was worth it. He wiped away his tears. Then he returned to his textbooks. He knew that the trials he faced now would ultimately shape him into the compassionate physician he aspired to be.

Final Exams and Triumph

Robert's final year was by far his toughest yet. Clinical rotations required long hours at hospitals, while his final exams seemed insurmountable. For weeks before these assessments, Robert devoted his time to reading books. He attended practical and hands-on mock clinical sessions. Robert also reviewed case studies with peers. The pressure was immense. He did not succumb to it. Instead, he found strength in the support of his friends. They shared in his struggles. Together, they followed a regular schedule. They alternated between intensive study sessions and moments of relaxation. This routine reinforced the bond that had flourished throughout their years in medical school.

Robert held his breath as his name appeared on the pass list. He had achieved his MBBS degree. A wave of relief and joy washed over him. He knew that all the hard work, sleepless nights, and sacrifices had culminated at this moment of triumph. As he celebrated with his friends, he realized that this was not just an end. It was the beginning of his journey into the medical field. He would make a difference in countless lives!

On that evening, Robert stood alone on campus. He gazed upon the clock tower of his university.

He whispered with pride and thanksgiving. "This is for you, Maple Grove."

He spoke with a heart full of gratitude. He reflected on the path that had led him here. He cherished the memories of late nights and early mornings that shaped his character. As he began to walk away, he felt a renewed sense of purpose. He knew that the real work of healing was just beginning. His chest began aching with pride as well as gratitude.

A Doctor is Born

With his degree in hand, Robert Carter officially entered adulthood as Dr. Robert Carter, a title that resonated deeply within him, signifying years of hard work, dedication, and dreams realized. As he stepped into his first day as an intern, the weight of responsibility settled on his shoulders. He also felt an exhilarating sense of possibility. He knew he was now equipped to make a tangible difference in the lives of others.

He was ready to take on the world and fulfill his promise of healing and service. He donned his white coat with pride and responsibility. He recognized it as a symbol of the trust placed in him by patients and society alike. The journey ahead would be daunting. He was prepared to face each challenge. He had cultivated compassion and dedication during his years of training.

CHAPTER 5

INTERNSHIP INSIGHTS

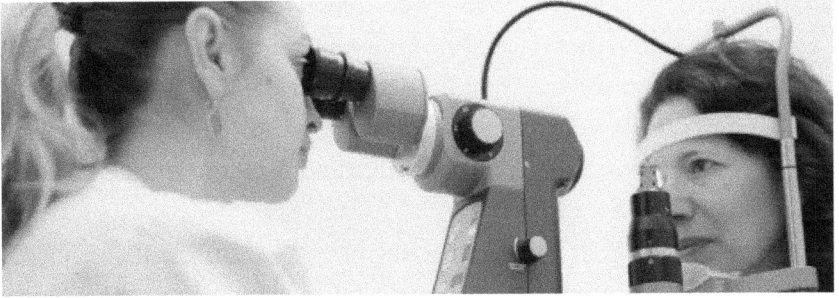

Excerpt

Robert Carter's internship journey in internal medicine and general surgery is marked by challenges and personal growth. His experiences taught him the importance of holistic patient care and the impact of empathy in medicine. He was inspired by mentors, particularly in cardiology. He aspires to innovate and enhance patient care through technology. He believes in a transformative future for the field.

The First Steps of Internal Medicine

Robert Carter began his internship in internal medicine, an area he had always found captivating. Each day presented new challenges, pushing him to apply the knowledge he had garnered over years of studying. Despite the busy patient rounds and complex cases, he felt a strong sense of purpose. He was determined to impact people's lives positively. Working at St. Anne's Hospital's busy wards quickly immersed him in patient care realities.

Long corridors echoed with the sound of ringing phones, hastened footsteps, and muffled consultations. The urgent conversations and fast pace made him keenly aware of his heavy responsibilities. Every patient interaction taught Robert to improve his diagnostic skills and build trusting, compassionate relationships. Robert observed senior residents to learn the art of patient interviews, clinical diagnoses and treatment plans.

One of his first patients, Mrs. Grayson, had come in with symptoms that seemed both vague and alarming. He sat down to talk about her concerns. He realized it involved understanding her fears and hopes, not just the medical facts. Mrs Grayson had uncontrolled diabetes with several symptoms and complications requiring a physician's care. Robert carefully reviewed Mrs. Grayson's charts, adjusted her medications, and offered comfort during challenging times to support her through this difficult period.

Dr. Patel told Robert that treating the disease wasn't enough. He needed to focus on the patient's overall wellness. This holistic approach inspired Robert to think about how lifestyle changes would help Mrs. Grayson improve her health. Together, they began discussing practical strategies for managing her condition while also nurturing her aspirations for the future.

These words echoed throughout his career as he responded to each case ranging from fevers to heart failure. His ability to connect with patients and eagerness to learn earned him respect from both patients and colleagues. With each interaction, he deepened his understanding of the intricate links between physical and mental health. He felt a strong need to promote comprehensive care that focused on treatments alongside support for personal growth.

The Demand of General Surgery

After six months, Robert transitioned into general surgery, an arena of precision and high stakes. The operating room has been transformed into his new classroom. Every procedure presented an opportunity to refine his skills and expand his medical knowledge. During his surgeries, he realized how deeply his decisions affected his patients' lives.

He learned the nuances of sutures, incisions, and post-operative care. Each successful operation bolstered his confidence, yet the weight of responsibility weighed heavily on his shoulders. He understood that mastery in this field was not just about technical ability. It also required empathy and effective communication with patients and their families.

Robert thrived under pressure, with early mornings and late nights becoming the new normal. He welcomed the challenge. He knew that every moment in the operating room brought him closer to his goal of being a skilled surgeon. He prioritized connecting with his patients, ensuring they felt heard and supported during their journeys. Each day posed its own unique challenges to his endurance and skill set.

One memorable incident took place during an emergency appendectomy. Robert used his training and intuition to manage unexpected complications. The successful outcome not only boosted his confidence but also reinforced his commitment to his patients' well-being. As the condition of a patient quickly worsened, Robert assisted the lead surgeon with firm hands and unwavering focus.

"You have an innate talent," commented the surgeon afterward. The compliment filled Robert with a sense of pride and validation for his hard work. It was moments like these that reminded him why he chose this challenging yet rewarding profession. The surgeon continued, "Have you considered becoming a specialist?"

Robert took great comfort from receiving praise, yet found himself drawn away to pursue another undertaking entirely. He had always been fascinated by medical research and the potential it held for advancing treatment options. He felt a surge of determination to explore new areas of medicine.

A Heartfelt Calling: Cardiology

Robert first came into contact with cardiology during his internal medicine rotation. He was captivated by the complexity of the heart and its vital role in overall health. As he shadowed the cardiologists, each patient interaction fueled his wish to delve deeper into this intricate field. Its intricate workings, rhythms, and vulnerabilities fascinated him greatly.

His admiration grew when he met Dr. Eleanor Hayes, a respected cardiologist and visiting professor known for her intelligence and kindness. Dr. Hayes explained complex cases and shared her passion for patient care, further inspiring Robert. He understood that cardiology involves building lasting relationships with patients and significantly improving their lives, not just treating heart issues.

One afternoon, she invited Robert to watch a cardiac catheterization procedure. As he watched the team work seamlessly together, he felt a surge of excitement and curiosity about the intricate process. This experience strengthened his commitment to a career in cardiology, where he can meaningfully impact people's lives. Standing by her side, he marveled at the precision and skill needed to navigate delicate arteries of the heart.

"Cardiology isn't just science," she declared with passion, her eyes widening with intensity. *"It's also an art, each heart tells its own unique tale, and it is our duty as cardiologists to listen."*

He nodded, captivated by her perspective. He realized that this blend of artistry and science resonated deeply with his aspirations. He felt he was exactly where he needed to be, ready to start a life-changing journey.

Robert knew instantly that he had found his calling. The prospect of mastering these complex procedures ignited a sense of exhilaration within him. He took a deep breath, ready to embrace the challenges ahead. With determination in his eyes, he envisioned the lives he would touch and help.

Inspired by Mentors

Eleanor Hayes wasn't the only influence on his journey. Dr. Alan Vickers, another cardiologist, often held lectures about innovations in cardiac care. His enthusiasm inspired Robert to go beyond conventional thinking in medicine and explore beyond basic treatments. Robert found himself drawn to the possibility of integrating technology into patient care. It was at that intersection of medicine and innovation that he felt he would truly make a difference.

"Why settle for treating one heart at a time when you can revolutionize cardiology? Dr. Vickers challenged his students.

These mentors greatly influenced Robert, sparking his interest in cardiology that would guide his future.

The Path Ahead

Robert was not just an intern. He had a strong vision and a deep commitment to understanding cardiology.

He reflected on his first year as a doctor and felt thankful for his patients. He appreciated his mentors and the opportunity to make a difference in people's lives. He realized that each experience had shaped his perspective and fueled his passion for the field. With a fresh determination, Robert got ready to face the challenges and opportunities in his medical career.

Now it was time for him to build on that legacy. He envisioned a future where technology seamlessly integrated with patient care, enhancing outcomes and accessibility. As he looked ahead, Robert was eager to create change and motivate others as he had been motivated.

He understood that the road ahead would not be easy, but the potential for innovation in cardiology fueled his ambition. With every step, he sought to connect traditional practices with groundbreaking advancements. He ensured that no heart was left behind.

CHAPTER 6

HEALING BEYOND MEDICINE: A DOCTOR'S SPIRITUAL JOURNEY

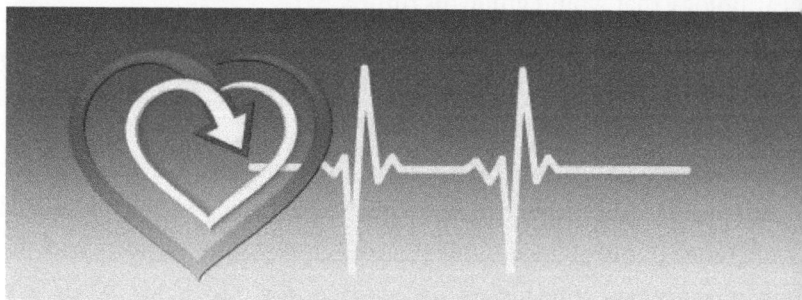

Excerpt

Dr. Robert Carter's journey through medical training highlights the profound connection between healing and spirituality. As he navigates the challenges of residency, he learns to balance work and family, finding solace in faith. This transformation enriches his practice, emphasizing compassion and understanding, ultimately shaping his approach to patient care and personal fulfillment.

Licensed to Heal

Dr. Robert Carter stood proudly before an audience full of graduates to recite the Hippocratic Oath together. This tradition signified a promise made to humanity with integrity and compassion in mind. As they raised their right hands together, they felt a strong sense of responsibility for their future roles. They realized their journey was not just about medicine. It was also about being a source of hope for those in need.

"Above all, do no harm," he repeated with reverence, mindful that his actions would either save lives or take them.

With each word, he saw the weight of their commitment sinking into the hearts of the new physicians. This moment marked the beginning of their mission to heal. They aimed to uplift the human spirit. True healing extends beyond prescriptions and procedures.

Robert felt both pride and responsibility upon receiving his medical license. Robert recognized that the challenges ahead would be even greater. He understood that the journey of a healer was fraught with uncertainty and required unwavering dedication. He was ready to tackle these challenges. His passion for medicine and hope for a better future for his patients motivated him.

Residency: A Baptism by Fire

Robert decided to specialize in cardiology, enrolling in an intense three-year residency program at St Anne's Hospital. From day one, its intensity became clear. The long hours and high-stakes environment were relentless, pushing him to his limits both mentally and physically. Yet, each experience deepened his resolve, igniting a fire within him that he had never felt before.

Robert worked long hours managing patient rounds, diagnostic tests, emergency procedures, and late-night on-call shifts for heart attack victims. These shifts tested his endurance and focus but proved invaluable to patient care. As he navigated the complexities of each case, Robert found himself becoming more adept at making quick decisions under pressure. With every successful intervention, his confidence grew, reinforcing his commitment to the demanding path he had chosen.

Robert's team urgently called him to help. A man in his 40s was suffering severe chest pain. He had fainted. Working diligently alongside his colleagues, Robert was committed to stabilizing and treating the patient. When the man finally regained consciousness, he reached out to shake Robert's hand and softly said, "Thank you, doctor. You have given me another chance at life."

Robert found comfort in moments like these, even when his workload seemed insurmountable. Each grateful acknowledgment reminded him of the profound impact he would have on the lives of others. It fueled his determination to push through the long nights and endless challenges that lay ahead.

Balancing Work and Family

Residency wasn't only a test of Robert's medical skills. It was also a test of balance. Juggling demanding hospital shifts with precious time spent at home required careful planning and unwavering dedication. Each evening, he walked through the door. His child's smile reminded him that every sacrifice was worth it. Married to Laura, Robert struggled to divide his time between work and family life.

Laura was Robert's steadfast pillar, skillfully managing their home while providing unwavering support. Yet, there were moments of tension as missed family dinners and long absences tested their relationship. Despite the challenges, they always found a way to communicate openly and reconnect, emphasizing the importance of their partnership. Each weekend, they spent quality time together. They created cherished memories. These moments strengthened their bond amid the chaos.

"Robert, don't forget we need you too." Laura would often remind Robert.

He remained mindful of her words, reminding himself to cherish every moment with loved ones no matter how brief. As the weeks went by, Robert prioritized scheduling regular family outings. He ensured that their time together was meaningful. Their outings were also enjoyable. These shared experiences brought laughter and joy into their lives. They also reaffirmed their commitment to nurturing their family ties.

A Divine Encounter

Robert experienced a divine encounter while immersed in residency's hustle and bustle. Not about his career trajectory, but rather in terms of his personal spiritual development. On an otherwise sleepless night, he felt overwhelmed with work demands. Personal responsibilities weighed heavily on him.

He found himself drawn towards the hospital chapel for solace. Inside the quiet sanctuary, he knelt in prayer, seeking clarity and comfort in the chaos surrounding him. At that moment of stillness, he felt an undeniable sense of peace wash over him. It ignited a renewed sense of purpose in both his professional and personal life.

Robert was in total silence as he contemplated his life, purpose, and burdens he carried with him. The flickering candlelight cast gentle shadows on the walls. It reminded him of the fleeting nature of time. He thought about the importance of cherishing each moment. He took a deep breath and realized that his burdens would also be sources of strength. This would happen if he chose to embrace them.

As he browsed his Bible randomly, his eyes caught Matthew 11:28.

It read, *'Come to Me all who are weary and burdened, and I will give you rest.'*

The words resonated deeply within him. They offered solace and a promise of relief from the weight he had been carrying. In that quiet moment, he resolved to let go of the past. He decided to seek the rest that had long eluded him. He embraced a path ahead with newfound hope.

Robert felt a sense of peace that he couldn't explain. This peace led him to attend church services. Over time, he studied the Bible. Gradually, he formed connections with others who shared his journey, finding strength in their community and faith. Each gathering felt like a reclamation of his spirit, reminding him that he was never truly alone in his struggles. With Laura's encouragement, Robert developed his newfound faith by surrendering his life to Christ.

Born Again

Becoming a Christian didn't make life any simpler. Yet, it provided Robert with a greater purpose beyond medicine. He saw his patients not just as cases, but as individuals created in God's image. This shift in perspective transformed his approach to healing, as he began to incorporate compassion and understanding into every interaction. He realized that faith was not just a belief to hold. It was a way of life. This enriched both his own existence and the lives of those around him.

Laura was delighted at his spiritual transformation. Together they began praying regularly. They sought God's guidance in every area of their lives. As their bond deepened through shared prayers and spiritual growth, they felt a draw to service. They started volunteering at local shelters and offered support to those in need. This commitment to helping others solidified their faith. It brought them closer together. It fostered a sense of community that enriched their lives far beyond what they had imagined.

A New Perspective

By the end of his residency, Robert had developed a profound new perspective on both his profession and personal life. He understood that healing extended beyond the physical, recognizing the importance of emotional and spiritual well-being in his patients' journeys. Robert had emerged not just as an experienced cardiologist but as someone transformed both spiritually and emotionally. His faith became the cornerstone of his life. It gave him renewed strength to serve both patients and family.

Robert was aware that as he moved ahead into his next phase of career, the challenges would only increase. Yet, with God on his side, he felt prepared to face whatever lay in store for him. He embraced each new opportunity with optimism. He knew that every patient contact would be a chance to make a meaningful impact. This commitment to compassionate care became the foundation of his future practice, guiding his interactions with both patients and colleagues.

CHAPTER 7

TRANSFORMING LIVES: A DAY WITH DR ROBERT CARTER

Excerpt

Dr. Robert Carter, a dedicated cardiologist, combines patient care, mentoring, and research to transform lives. With a passion for healing, he thrives in emergency scenarios while imparting knowledge to future physicians. His commitment extends beyond hospital walls through community health programs, emphasizing the importance of compassionate medicine and heart health awareness.

The Heartbeat of a Healer

Dr. Robert Carter had always been fascinated by the intricate workings of the human heart. After years of hard work in medical school, he turned his passion into a lifelong commitment to healing.

Robert took pride in being one of the leading cardiologists, embracing his new role with enthusiasm and determination. Every day posed new challenges, from saving lives in emergency situations to mentoring the next generation of physicians.

Hospitals became his second homes, and catheterization labs or "cath labs" served as his battleground against heart-related mysteries. In those cath labs, Robert experienced the thrill of discovery. He also faced the weight of responsibility. He knew that each procedure would mean the difference between life and death for his patients.

He often thought about the stories behind each heartbeat. He reminded himself that every diagnosis signifies a unique life deserving compassion and care. Here he took on one patient at a time to confront these mysteries of our circulatory systems and discover solutions. Each success renewed his sense of purpose and strengthened his dedication to exploring cardiology further. Seeing his patients recover and reclaim their lives reminded him why he chose this path.

Saving Lives in Real Time

Robert was often at the frontline of cardiology emergencies. Heart attacks, arrhythmias, and other cardiac emergencies demand quick thinking and decisive action from him. These were common scenarios requiring immediate medical care. He improved his skills with each case. He learned to stay calm under pressure. He recognized the significant impact his actions would have on patients' futures. The adrenaline rush that accompanied these emergency situations fueled his passion for the field even more.

One memorable case was Mr. Thompson, an elderly man who came to the emergency room with chest pain, showing signs of a heart attack. Within minutes, Robert took him into the cath lab. They performed emergency angioplasty and stent placement to unblock an artery. The artery had become blocked. The relief on Mr. Thompson's face after the procedure was a profound reminder of the importance of their work. Each successful intervention not only saved a life but also reinforced Robert's commitment to his calling as a healthcare provider.

As blood flow was restored and monitors stabilized, Mr. Thompson's life was saved. Mr. Thompson tearfully described Robert as responsible, holding his hand tightly during their goodbye hug. Robert smiled, feeling a sense of fulfillment wash over him as he watched Mr. Thompson leave with his family. Moments like these reignited his passion and reminded him why he chose this challenging but rewarding path.

These moments reaffirmed Robert's passion for his work despite its heavy burden of responsibility. Every life he helped to save became a testament to his dedication and skill. Robert took a deep breath, prepared for the next challenge. He felt a renewed sense of purpose, realizing his efforts would truly impact someone's life. He felt invigorated, ready to tackle the challenges that lay ahead.

Teaching the Next Generation

Robert's passion for cardiology extended far beyond patient care. He wanted to share his knowledge with aspiring doctors, hoping to inspire them like his mentors inspired him. He shared his extensive knowledge with medical students and residents. He provided them with valuable insights he had gained over the years. Through lectures and hands-on training sessions, he emphasized the importance of empathy and compassion in medicine. Robert believed that with the right guidance, these future physicians would excel in their careers. They would also make a meaningful difference in the lives of their patients.

"Medicine is more than science," he would tell his students during ward rounds. "It requires compassion, communication and the courage to make difficult decisions."

He quickly became well-known at St. Anne's Medical School for his engaging teaching style, which helped students understand complex cardiology concepts through examples and real-life situations. His innovative approach inspired many students to pursue careers in cardiology. He created a new generation of doctors eager to make a positive impact. Many of his former students would often return to express their gratitude. They shared stories of how his mentorship shaped their paths in medicine.

Pioneering Research

Robert found immense pleasure in research, delving deeply into cardiac health and treatment. His dedication led to several groundbreaking studies that challenged existing norms and offered new insights into patient care. His work gained recognition. He became a sought-after speaker at conferences. There, he shared his findings and encouraged collaboration among fellow researchers. His pioneering studies on innovative stent designs and non-invasive diagnostic techniques earned him immense acclaim among his peers.

Research was an arduous yet satisfying effort. He faced many challenges. These challenges only fueled his passion further. Each success inspired him to push the boundaries of medical knowledge. Robert believed that through ongoing research, the future of cardiac care would be transformed for countless patients worldwide. Long hours spent analyzing data were balanced by the excitement of publishing findings that would improve patient outcomes.

Life in the Cath lab

Robert discovered peace amid the rhythms of his Cath Lab. Here, he conducted lifesaving procedures like angioplasties, stent placements and pacemaker insertions, procedures which saved lives every day. The beeping monitors and the focused energy of his colleagues created an atmosphere charged with purpose and determination. In this space, Robert felt an unwavering commitment to his patients. He also had the drive to innovate within the ever-evolving field of cardiology.

"Working in the cath lab is like being a pilot," he often noted. "Every step must be precise, leaving no room for mistakes.

Robert thrived under pressure in this high-tech environment. His hands moved deftly. Years of training guided them. An innate sense of rhythm made complex maneuvers effortless. Each successful procedure allowed him to heal hearts. He also strengthened his resolve to push the boundaries of cardiac care. Each successful procedure was seen as a win in his ongoing fight against cardiovascular disease.

A Day in the Life of a Cardiologist

Robert was kept busy from dawn to dusk. Each morning began with hospital rounds. He checked on patients recovering from surgeries or procedures. He helped patients overcome physical limitations after treatment or procedures. His warm demeanor and reassuring presence put their minds at ease. This fostered a crucial sense of trust for their recovery. He moved from room to room. He listened intently to their concerns. He was ready to offer both medical skill and emotional support.

Midday, he would switch over to the catheter lab, performing scheduled interventions or handling emergency cases. The day's rhythm pulsed with urgency. He navigated through a series of critical situations. He adapted quickly to the needs of each patient. Despite the demanding pace, Robert found fulfillment in every heartbeat. Each life he touched was significant to him. He knew that his dedication made a tangible difference. Evenings were spent preparing lectures or catching up with medical research.

Even during his hectic workdays, Robert always made time for family and faith. He cherished these moments of connection, understanding that a balanced life was essential to maintaining his passion for medicine. His family's love gave him the foundation he needed. Their support helped him face the challenges of his demanding career each day. Evening prayers with Laura and their three children became an important ritual. These prayers helped keep Robert grounded, despite an unpredictable career path.

The Call of the Heart

Robert found purpose in his lifelong calling as a cardiologist through both its highs and lows. Each patient saved, each student mentored, and each discovery in the laboratory furthered his calling. The thrill of innovation drove his passion. The joy of seeing his patients thrive reminded him of why he had chosen this path. Through every challenge, Robert remained steadfast, determined to bridge the gap between advanced medical technology and compassionate care.

Robert Carter made cardiology his life mission and demonstrated it by healing hearts both physically and spiritually. He believed that medicine was not just about treating ailments, but about nurturing the human spirit. With a heart full of gratitude, he embraced each day as an opportunity to make a meaningful impact on the lives of those around him

His commitment extended beyond the hospital walls. He volunteered in community health programs. He strives to educate the public about heart health and prevention. Robert shared his knowledge and experiences. He aimed to inspire others. This created a ripple effect of awareness that would save lives before they even stepped foot in his clinic.

CHAPTER 8

INTEGRATING FAITH AND MEDICINE: MERGING THEOLOGY AND CARDIOLOGY

Excerpt

Dr. Robert Carter started a transformative journey. He aimed to integrate faith with medicine. He believed in the holistic healing of body and spirit. After two years of theological studies, he returned to cardiology, blending spiritual practices into patient care. This approach fostered deeper connections and enhanced recovery, embodying his commitment to serve humanity comprehensively.

Sabbatical leave

Dr. Robert Carter had always believed in the healing power of both the body and the spirit. His years of practice had shown him how profound the effects of faith would be in a patient's recovery. Sitting in silence in his office, he felt a strong restlessness urging him to explore his beliefs more deeply. He realized it was the perfect time to start a transformative journey. This journey would combine his medical skills with a deep exploration of faith.

Despite colleagues' warnings, Robert contemplated leaving medicine temporarily to enroll in a two-year theology program at a Bible school. He anticipated that this change would improve his ability to help others.

Upon completing his residency in cardiology, Robert found himself at a critical crossroads. He refined his skills as a physician for years. He felt a deep calling to explore the spiritual truths that had guided his path.

He decided to take a 2 year Sabbatical leave. This time away would intertwine his medical skill with a profound exploration of faith and healing. This quest promised to transform his practice. It would also enrich the lives of those he served in unimaginable ways.

A New Classroom

Gone were the operating rooms and lecture halls filled with medical charts. Instead, Robert found himself surrounded by theologians, pastors, and students who shared his thirst for understanding divine truths. He found a deep sense of purpose in biblical teachings that he couldn't find in the clinical world. Each class broadened his perspective. It prompted him to integrate his medical knowledge with spiritual insights. This transformation reshaped his understanding of healing.

He explored church history, biblical exegesis, hermeneutics, pastoral care, and missions, among other subjects. He honed his skills in writing academic essays, conducting biblical research, and crafting compelling theses. As his confidence grew, Robert began to see the connections between science and faith more clearly. He recognized that both would coexist harmoniously in the pursuit of truth. With each passing day, he felt an increasing urge to share this newfound wisdom. He was eager to bridge the gap between medicine and ministry.

He actively engaged with the campus community, interacted with fellow students, and forged strong bonds that led to lasting friendships. Through group discussions and collaborative projects, Robert discovered diverse perspectives that enriched his own understanding and sparked meaningful conversations. He realized that this journey involved integrating these realms. It was as much about personal growth as it was about impacting the lives of those around him.

Robert transformed his perception of healthcare. He acknowledged that patients are more than mere physical entities in need of treatment.

They are whole individuals worthy of compassion, empathy, and profound spiritual connections. This holistic approach fundamentally revolutionized his practice. It enabled him to cultivate a deep sense of empathy. This empathy transcended the boundaries of conventional medicine.

With each interaction, Robert wholeheartedly embraced the immense responsibility that accompanied his newfound understanding. He came to recognize that genuine healing involves not just the mind but also the spirit. This transformative journey sparked a deep passion within him. He wanted to integrate the fields of medicine and ministry. This passion inspired him to create a holistic healing approach that nourishes the body, soul, and the spirit.

The Bible school awakened a transformative perspective within him, enabling him to view the world through the lens of faith. He began to see each patient not just as a case to be treated. He saw them as a soul in need of care and compassion. This profound insight drove him to develop workshops that merged medical knowledge with spiritual guidance, promoting a comprehensive wellness experience.

He immersed himself in courses on biblical interpretation, church history, and systematic theology. Through these studies, he broadened his understanding in profoundly unexpected ways. He approached the scriptures with meticulous attention, dissecting verses with the same precision he once applied to analyzing EKG readings.

He had an innovative perspective. It allowed him to intertwine the rhythms of the heart with the spiritual flow of life. This significantly enhanced his empathy for those he sought to heal. As he delved deeper, he discovered how faith and medicine would coexist, each enriching the other in remarkable ways.

This newfound synergy became the cornerstone of his practice. It inspired both his patients and colleagues to embrace a more holistic approach to healing. As he integrated these insights into his practice, he began to envision a pioneering program. In this program, medical professionals and spiritual leaders would collaborate to offer holistic care to their communities.

The Heart and the Soul

As Robert delved into his studies, he began to draw intriguing parallels between medicine and theology. He discovered that both fields sought to understand the complexities of human existence. They offer comfort and solutions to life's most profound challenges. This realization fueled his passion to create workshops. These workshops would bridge the gap between science and spirituality. They aimed to foster a collaborative environment for learning and growth.

In medicine, he learned to chart the complexities of the physical heart, diagnosing its ailments and restoring its vital rhythm. In theology, he explored the deeper significance of the soul, seeking to heal emotional wounds and nurture inner peace. By uniting these disciplines, Robert aimed to craft a transformative healing experience that honored the body, soul and

spirit. He uncovered the profound intricacies of the human soul and the essential quest for spiritual healing.

One of his professors once remarked, "The human heart can only be truly whole when the soul finds its peace."

With this wisdom guiding him, Robert devoted himself to understanding the delicate interplay between physical health and spiritual well-being. His journey proved that true healing transcends mere symptom relief. It embraces the entirety of human existence. Those words stayed with Robert. They reminded him that his calling was not an abandonment of one field for another. It was a merging of both.

Trials and Triumphs

Through prayer and reflection, Robert found a deepening resolve. He realized that this path was essential. It was not only crucial for his faith but also for his future as a healer. He recognized that each challenge was an opportunity for growth, both personally and professionally. Robert embraced his studies with renewed vigor. He began to witness the transformative power of healing rituals. He also noticed their impact on those he encountered.

After two years of intense study, Robert graduated with a Master of Theology. With his newfound knowledge, he stepped into the world. He was ready to make a difference and eager to apply his insights in practical settings. The journey ahead promised many opportunities. He would intertwine faith and healing. He aimed to guide others on their own paths toward wholeness. Standing on the stage to get his degree, he felt a deep sense of fulfillment.

It wasn't just another title to add to his name. It represented the culmination of 2 years of dedication. It also showed his heartfelt commitment to his mission. As he held his degree, he envisioned the countless lives he would touch. He was forever inspired by the profound connections between mind, body, and spirit.

With each new understanding, Robert longed to create spaces where individuals would explore and heal holistically. He knew that the road ahead would be filled with obstacles, but his conviction to empower others fueled his determination.. It was a testament to his commitment to understanding and serving humanity in a holistic way.

Returning to the Stethoscope

Armed with his newfound theological insights, Robert returned to cardiology with a renewed purpose. He aimed to integrate spiritual practices into medical care. He wanted to offer patients treatments for their physical ailments. He also intended to give support for their emotional and spiritual well-being.

Robert began to implement this holistic approach. He saw remarkable shifts in his patients' attitudes towards their recovery. This change ignited a deeper understanding of the healing process. Medicine had taught him how to treat the body. Theology had shown him how to minister to the soul and spirit.

His conversations with patients now carried a deeper resonance. He saw beyond their physical symptoms to their fears, hopes, and struggles.

He shared the Gospel and prayed with those who were open to it. He offered words of encouragement to those in despair.

For Robert, this blending of medicine and faith became the cornerstone of his practice. He wasn't just a cardiologist or a theologian. He was a bridge between two worlds. He mapped both the heart and the soul with every life he touched.

This chapter in Robert's odyssey was a reminder. Sometimes, stepping away from one path can lead to a richer journey. It can also lead to a more meaningful journey.

CHAPTER 9

FROM HEALING TO HOPE: A DOCTOR'S INSPIRATIONAL STORY

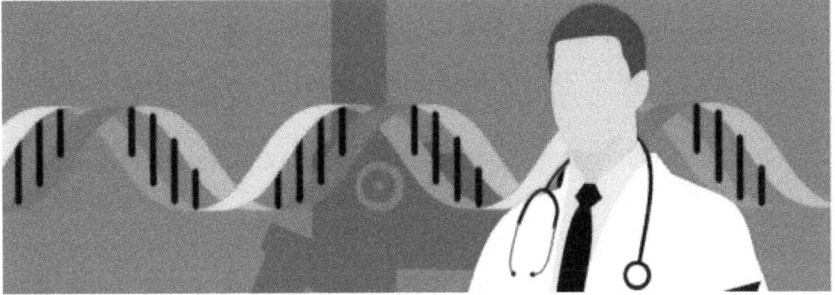

Excerpt

Dr. Robert Carter's transition from hospital medicine to private practice fostered a legacy of hope through personalized and holistic care. After a diving accident left him paralyzed, he underwent a miraculous recovery, ultimately retiring to focus on community service. His journey exemplifies resilience, inspiring others to find strength in adversity and embrace new ministries.

Building a Legacy in Private Practice

After years in hospitals and academia, Dr. Robert Carter took the exciting step into solo private practice. For two decades, his clinic served as a beacon of hope to many patients throughout his community. Dr. Carter transformed local healthcare by prioritizing personalized care and building strong relationships with his patients. He treated ailments and emphasized holistic well-being, building trust and a sense of belonging among those he served.

The office was filled with the sounds of medical devices, rustling patient files, and soft consultations. He would practice medicine his way, emphasizing holistic care alongside physical healing. His approach not only addressed immediate health concerns but also encouraged lifestyle changes that fostered overall wellness. Many patients not only recovered but also thrived under his guidance. They often returning to share their success stories and express gratitude.

A Market Place Ministry

Robert saw his clinic as more than just an office. It was his mission field or "marketplace ministry," enabling him to share God's love in subtle and meaningful ways.

"My clinic is my pulpit," he would declare. "My staffs and patients are my congregation."

He offered encouragement and comfort to patients in need. Many patients found solace not only from his medical skill but also his genuine care for their spiritual well-being. Robert created an environment where hope thrived, making every interaction an opportunity to uplift those around him. He often hosted prayer sessions for his staff, fostering a sense of community that extended beyond the clinic's walls. He shared the Gospel message and the love of Christ with his staff, patients, and visitors.

One elderly patient, Mrs. Thompson, often reminisced about her youth as she listened to Robert's uplifting words. She felt a renewed sense of purpose. She also felt a sense of belonging. This brought a sparkle to her eyes and a warmth to her heart.

Mrs Thompson, thanked Dr. Carter with tears after an annual check-up and thanked him profusely: "You don't just heal hearts, Dr. Carter; you mend souls!"

The unforeseen Accident

Life in private practice was satisfying but never without its challenges. One summer while vacationing with his family, Robert decided to go diving, something he had enjoyed doing since childhood. He plunged into the clear blue waters. He felt a unique sense of freedom. Only the ocean would offer such excitement. An unexpected accident turned his joyful adventure into a struggle for survival as he was caught in a sudden current.

What started as a harmless game turned tragic. Robert misjudged the water's depth. This mistake resulted in a fractured neck, severe pain, and paralysis. He required immediate medical attention at a nearby hospital. Doctors diagnosed a severe cervical fracture with spinal cord injury. They would only offer spinal surgery as the only workable solution. There were no guarantees for a positive outcome. As Robert lay in the hospital bed, he couldn't help but think about how quickly life can change. He was determined to overcome the challenges ahead and regain his love for diving. He underwent emergency spinal surgery. The process was exhausting. It made him physically tired and emotionally exposed. Yet, he drew strength from the support of his family, pastors, church members, and friends. With each passing day of recovery, Robert embraced physical therapy with a fierce determination, eager to reclaim his former self.

A Miraculous Recovery

Although physical therapy sessions were painful and progress was slow, his faith kept him strong through it all. Each small victory in therapy reignited a sense of hope in him, bringing back the joy he once experienced underwater. He eagerly imagined the thrill of diving deep into the ocean again.

Friends, family, and former patients rallied behind him and offered their prayers of strength. Their support became a source of inspiration, reminding him that he was never alone in his journey. As Robert faced challenges, he began to dream of swimming and exploring the colorful coral reefs and marine life. Laura would remind him of that during an especially trying day: "God isn't done with you yet!"

Robert defied all odds to experience a remarkable recovery and was capable of walking again. Robert's doctors were amazed, calling it miraculous. For Robert, it was evidence of God's grace and faithfulness. With newfound motivation, he continued physical therapy with a determination he had never felt before.

The Decision to Retire

Robert's accident and recovery made him reassess his priorities. It prompted him to make the tough decision to leave medical practice. He decided to retire from practice altogether. After much prayer and contemplation, this difficult decision was ultimately reached and approved. He knew it was time to focus on his health and explore new opportunities. Embracing this change, Robert set out to find purpose in serving his community in different ways.

"It's time to focus on a different ministry," he advised Laura.

Though Robert left his clinic job, his mission of faith and healing continued. He became more active in his church. He started mentoring young doctors. He shared his faith and healing story with congregations and community groups. His passion for helping others grew stronger as he discovered new avenues to support those in need. Robert felt invigorated, knowing that each conversation and each mentor session was making a difference in someone's life.

A New Chapter Begins

Robert's retirement was not an end but a new chapter for him. His experiences as a doctor gave him a deeper sense of purpose. The challenges he faced also contributed to this purpose. He embraced volunteer work, dedicating his time to free health clinics and outreach programs aimed at underprivileged populations. With every act of service, he realized that healing was not just about medicine but also about compassion and connection.

A diving accident would have ended his journey. Instead, it became a turning point. It showed that miracles can happen even in life's darkest moments. Robert realized that resilience was essential for healing, both for himself and for those he assisted. With newfound enthusiasm, he committed to sharing his story, inspiring others to find strength in adversity. Through workshops and speeches, he reached diverse audiences, encouraging them to view challenges as opportunities for growth. Every shared experience added to his mission, creating a tapestry of hope and determination for everyone who listened.

CHAPTER 10
EMBRACING DIGITAL CREATIVITY IN WRITING

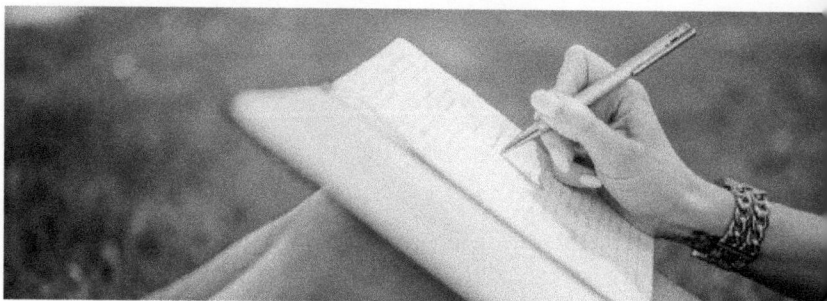

Excerpt

Dr. Robert Carter's transition from cardiologist to author reflects his passion for storytelling and mentorship. Through writing, he connects deeply with readers, inspiring them to find their own voices. He utilizes digital platforms to share insights, fostering a supportive community. His legacy is one of empowerment, hope, and creativity through words.

Discovering the Power of Words

Dr. Robert Carter's retirement allowed him to share what he knows, his experiences, and his beliefs through writing. What began as an outlet became a passion-fueled career. He built a career as an author. His stories resonated with readers. They captured the essence of human experience and emotion. With each book, he sought to inspire others to find their own voice. He encouraged them to embrace the transformative power of words. Dr. Carter understood that writing was not just about storytelling; it was about connecting with others on a deeper level. His dedication inspired many aspiring authors to explore their own stories and succeed in the literary world.

Robert started writing his memoir about his journey from a rural town to becoming a renowned cardiologist. The memoir received an overwhelmingly positive response. This encouragement motivated him to explore various genres over time. These genres included devotionals, travels, poetry, and self-help guides. He also delved into inspirational fiction. With each new genre, Robert discovered unique ways to express his thoughts and experiences, enriching his writing repertoire. His ability to weave profound insights into relatable narratives continued to captivate readers, solidifying his place in the literary community.

He quickly realized he had written 40 books, each offering its own message of hope, resilience, and purpose. Robert felt grateful for the support he received from his readers throughout his journey as an author. This realization sparked his passion for writing and inspired him to give back through workshops and mentorship for aspiring writers. The depth of his work resonated with a diverse audience, creating a loyal group that eagerly awaited each new release. As he reflected on his journey, Robert felt grateful for the opportunity to inspire others through the power of words.

Mentoring Aspiring Writers

As Robert's reputation as an author grew, he found great satisfaction in assisting new writers. He helped them improve their storytelling and understand the publishing process. He spent his weekends hosting workshops to share valuable insights and practical tips he had learned over the years. With each session, he saw his students' talent blossom. This fueled his own creativity. It also reminded him of the joy that comes from nurturing a passion for writing.

"Writing is an act of service," he would teach his students. *"It's about sharing your story to empower others."*

Robert provided many individuals with the tools they needed to bring their ideas to life. He did this through workshops, online courses, and consultations with him. His dedication to mentoring became a cornerstone of his legacy. He encouraged them to express their unique voices. He also encouraged their perspectives. The enthusiasm of his students rekindled his own love for storytelling. It reminded him that every narrative holds the potential to inspire change. His coaching extended far beyond simply writing mechanics. Rather it delved deeper into storytelling techniques and authenticity issues.

Embracing Digital Creativity

Robert also took advantage of digital platforms to write engaging social media content. He provided bite-sized lessons on writing, faith, and personal growth. Through these platforms, he managed to reach a broader audience, igniting passion in aspiring writers from diverse backgrounds. Each post sparked conversations that transcended geographical boundaries, creating a vibrant community of learners united by their love for storytelling.

Robert amassed an avid fan base through his podcasts, blogs, and newsletters, becoming a digital creator in his own right. His digital presence provided thoughtful blog posts. It also included quick tutorials on writing techniques. This variety became an incredible source of motivation to a global audience. He cultivated an atmosphere of encouragement, where individuals felt empowered to share their own stories and insights. This exchange of ideas enriched his content. It also fostered a sense of belonging among writers. These writers once felt isolated in their journeys.

A Legacy Through Words

Robert's life as an author and digital creator wasn't simply a job. It was an act of ministry. He dedicated himself to uplifting others, using his platform to inspire creativity and connect people across vast distances. He left a lasting legacy through every word he wrote. His legacy transcended the pages of his books. It resonated in the hearts of aspiring writers everywhere. Every book, blog post, or coaching session offered a chance to change lives forever. Each effort would leave behind something beautiful.

Robert realized his years as a cardiologist had prepared him for this new phase in his life. Before, he would physically heal hearts. Now, he sought to inspire and heal people through words. In embracing this new chapter, he found solace. He knew that his experiences and insights would guide others on their journeys. He fostered a community built on encouragement and support.

Each story shared became a beacon of hope, illuminating the path for those who dared to dream. With each passing day, Robert immersed himself deeper into storytelling. His creativity flowed freely. It inspired others. As he penned his thoughts, he discovered the true power of his words. They would connect souls across time and space. This created a tapestry of human experience that would uplift the spirit.

CHAPTER 11
CRISIS IN THE SKY

The Doctor's Dilemma: An Retired Physician's Journey through Crisis
Excerpt

A retired doctor is called to action as he must rely on his past skills to save a life during his travels. This captivating tale delves into themes of courage, resilience, and the journey of rediscovering one's purpose amidst an exhilarating adventure! He discovers that medicine is not just about healing the body, but also involves deeper aspects of care and understanding through unexpected challenges and self-reflection. Unraveling the layers of his past, he embarks on a profound quest for understanding and redemption.

A Peaceful Retirement

Dr. Robert Carter had enjoyed his retirement five years ago, living a calm life in his seaside home, gardening, reading novels, and traveling. His days were punctuated by the soothing rhythm of the waves and the warmth of the sun on his face. Yet, beneath the tranquil surface, he felt a lingering void, a whisper that adventure still awaited him beyond the horizon.

On a crisp autumn morning, Robert excitedly boarded a flight to Barcelona for a vacation he had eagerly awaited. His trip included plans for art, history, and relaxation, but he didn't realize it would lead to a deep rediscovery of his life's true purpose.

A Sudden Crisis

As the plane flew across the Atlantic Ocean, an unforeseen disturbance shattered the tranquility of his flight. A man in his late fifties suddenly collapsed in a nearby aisle, his skin glistening with a pale sheen of sweat. Robert was surprised by the sudden interruption of his peaceful journey and looked away in shock. However, the muffled cries for help stirred something within him, prompting Robert to rise from his seat.

"Is there a doctor on board?" the flight attendant called out, her voice filled with urgency.

Robert paused, contemplating whether to stay silent. After all, he was retired. Seeing the fear in the attendant's eyes and her helplessness among the panicking passengers, he decided to speak up.

Robert cast aside his uncertainties and firmly declared, "I am a doctor."

Instantly, the surrounding chaos began to settle as people turned their attention toward him. He took a deep breath, quickly assessing the situation, ready to take control of the unfolding crisis.

Drawing on Old Skills

Robert quickly scanned the scene: a passenger was unconscious with a weak pulse, so he called for a medical kit and oxygen as flight attendants rushed to help. He knelt beside the patient, gripping the urgency of the moment as it coursed through him. Every ounce of his energy was dedicated to reviving this individual and restoring his consciousness.

Robert suspected a cardiac event upon evaluating the man's airway, breathing, and circulation. After confirming ventricular fibrillation, he quickly used the onboard AED to deliver a shock and began CPR with expert precision. The seconds felt like minutes as he maintained the rhythm, urging the man's heart to respond. With each compression, Robert focused on reviving the life in that body, hoping for any sign of recovery.

Time stretched endlessly, but finally, the man regained consciousness, his breathing stabilizing and his color gradually returning. A wave of relief washed over Robert, yet his heart raced with an exhilarating sense of anticipation.

He had fought against the odds and won, but he knew the journey to full recovery was just beginning. Robert felt a deep bond with the man he had just saved, realizing their lives were forever linked by this moment.

An Unexpected Revelation

As Robert monitored the man on the flight, he eventually sank back into his seat, trembling hands betraying his turmoil. He was utterly spent, both physically and emotionally, by the harrowing experience. Despite having not performed CPR in years, his instincts surged forth in that critical moment, guiding him through the challenge.

The adrenaline rush was wearing off, leaving a wave of exhaustion washing over him. Looking out at the passing clouds, he sensed that this encounter would change him in ways he couldn't fully understand yet.

Later, Greg conveyed his deep gratitude for his rescue, stating, "Thank you," with genuine sincerity evident in his voice.

As Robert met the grateful gaze of Greg, a wave of conflicting emotions washed over him. At that moment, he truly understood how deeply he missed the powerful influence of his work as a doctor. Saving Greg had rekindled a flame within him that he had feared was extinguished forever.

The realization struck him that he could no longer ignore the calling to help others. Embracing this newfound inspiration, he vowed to realign his life with the values that had once defined his very existence.

Facing His Own Dilemma

Robert couldn't shake the memory of the incident that occurred during his trip. While exploring the lively streets and famous landmarks of Barcelona, he felt both fulfilled and conflicted. Had he made the mistake of retiring too soon?

The vibrant energy of the city reminded him of the purpose he had almost forgotten. While walking by street performers and artists, he felt that he still had an important role to fulfill in the world.

Robert thought leaving medicine would bring him peace, but his flight experience revealed a strong desire to help others. Is there a possibility for Robert to re-enter the field, even for a short time?

He couldn't shake the feeling that perhaps his journey in medicine wasn't entirely over. He imagined how he could still make a difference, reigniting the passion that once defined his life with every step he took.

A New Purpose

Once back home, Robert sought opportunities to leverage his medical skills without committing to full-time practice. He chose to volunteer at a local clinic, dedicating a few days each week to providing his expertise. This experience proved to be profoundly fulfilling, enabling him to reconnect with patients and significantly impact their lives.

Each interaction filled him with gratitude and purpose, helping him rediscover his identity. He realized that the power of healing extends beyond physical ailments to include compassion, understanding, and human connection.

Robert mentored medical students, sharing his knowledge and experiences to nurture future doctors. This effort enhanced their education and renewed his sense of purpose, enabling him to enjoy retirement while still staying connected to the medical field.

He often gathered with colleagues to discuss evolving practices and the latest advancements in medicine, fostering a sense of community. Robert experienced a constant sharing of wisdom that enhanced his life and the lives of his mentees.

Lessons Learned

Robert learned several important lessons from his flying experience, including:

Skill Never Truly Fade

Years into retirement, Robert found that his medical knowledge still resonated within him. This incident served as a poignant reminder that expertise and experience endure despite the passage of time. He realized that the foundation he had built over decades remained a powerful resource he could draw upon. This inspired him to mentor young professionals, building their confidence in their medical careers.

Purpose Is Ever-Evolving

Robert realized that retirement didn't equate to relinquishing his passions. Rather, it offered him the opportunity to redefine them and contribute in innovative ways. He started offering online workshops and community seminars to share his knowledge with more people. This shift reignited his purpose and helped him connect with people from various backgrounds, enriching his experiences and insights.

Courage in Uncertainty

Robert realized that to genuinely save Greg, he had to face his own fears directly. He understood that real courage stems from self-belief, particularly during moments of doubt and uncertainty. This journey transformed him and inspired others to face their challenges with resilience.

Conclusion

Dr. Robert Carter's experience during a crisis demonstrated his exceptional abilities and the importance of his life's mission. He not only successfully saved Greg's life during a critical emergency but also rekindled his deep-rooted passion for medicine. He reaffirmed his commitment to helping others, realizing that every life saved reflects his dedication. Robert emerged not just as a healer, but as a beacon of hope for those in need.

Robert's journey stands as a profound reminder that our talents and vocations never fade; they merely evolve. His "doctor's dilemma" became a catalyst for self-discovery, demonstrating that even in retirement, life can present astonishing and transformative experiences. During his journey, he found new ways to connect with the community and inspired others to follow their own healthcare paths. Robert revitalized his spirit and inspired those around him, creating a ripple effect beyond his immediate influence.

THE END

POEM 1

MAPPING THE HEART: A DOCTOR'S ODYSSEY

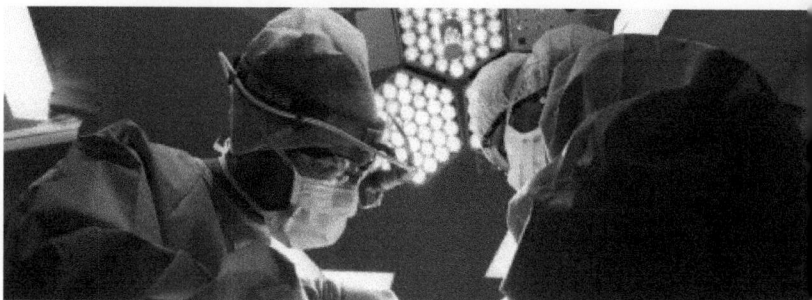

The unknown paths that life takes you on.
   The seeds of healing hope are planted by a healer.
   From rural roots to urban lights
   Sleepless nights are the foundation of a journey.
   Dreams take flight in lecture halls
   Through day and night, the hours go on forever.
   His art was the human heart.
   Map each part to heal, mend and map.
   Every beat tells a story
   The courage to be bold, the renewal of lives.
   His trusted guide is a stethoscope
   Hope is found in the midst of storms and pain.
   The heart would still yearn for more.
   Turn your souls towards eternal truths
   He found grace in healing the bodies.
   A sacred place, for a higher love.
   Quiet prayer from the eyes of patients
   The doctor's journey is revealed.
   Inspire, not just repair.

Light the world up with holy fire
Now, words are replacing the blade's edge.
His pen is a solemn promise of a healer.
His map grows through books and stories.
To lead new hearts to distant lands.
The journey is the art of this life.
Maps are not only for the flesh,
But also for the heart.

POEM 2

A DAY IN THE LIFE OF A CARDIOLOGIST

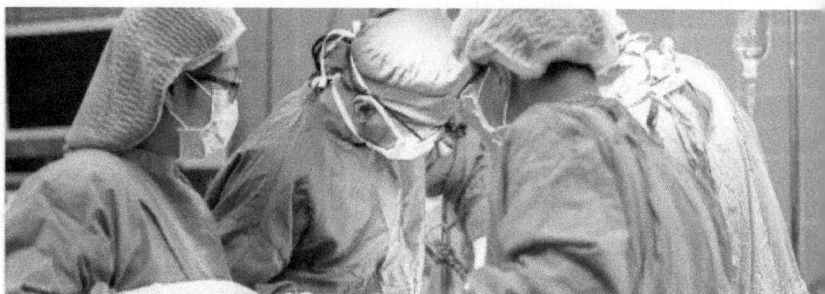

Pagers ring in the morning.
    It's another day.
    The white coat is ready and the stethoscope is in hand.
    Understanding is the key to healing your heart.
    The clinics are the places where these stories unfold.
    Fear, pain and courage are bold.
    Listening close to murmurs deep,
    Secrets that the beating heart can keep
    An echo hums, a rhythm tells,
    A dance of highs and lows.
    A little flutter, a pause or a skip.
    Soft words from the heart on the lips.
    The cath lab glow is now in full force.
    When urgency and skill are required.
    The vessel is freed by threading the wire.
    Moments when life and time progress.
    The charts are a combination of scans, calls and charts.
    Quiet prayer in the heart.
    For each decision, each repair,

A silent wish, a whispered concern
The pager begins to chime as the night falls.
Another Life, another Time
The sacred work continues.
All fragile hearts must be held.
Every heartbeat is a reminder of the importance of embracing life.
Cardiologists give their best.
The pulse of the divine guardian
Every heart contains a sacred symbol.

POEM 3

THE MAKING OF A DOCTOR

It all starts with a small spark or a vision in your mind.
Heal, help and serve the humankind.
The journey begins with textbooks and exams
Persistence is the key to success on a path of hard work.
The mind is stretched after long nights of studying
Anatomy's deepest levels, where wonders begin.
The veins, the heart and the lungs.
The source of all life's complexity is the marvellous wonder.
They toil in lecture halls and laboratories.
Sweat and soil are the result of failures and successes.
The steady hand is the scalpel edge
They are attempting to master the healing art.
Sleepless nights in hospital floors
Learning knocks at the door of your mind.
Each patient a teacher, each case a guide,
Build their confidence, their knowledge and their strength.
Every tear increases compassion.
They feel the pain of those they touch.
The heart of a healer begins to blossom.
Light that shines in the darkness.
Next comes the sacred vow or oath.

Never bow down when serving with honor.
A doctor's success is not just about skill.
It is heart and courage.
The journey is long and the call steep.
The rewards are great, and the meaning is deep.
To mend and restore is the purpose of life.
Heal the wounded forevermore.

POEM 4

THE POWER OF WORDS

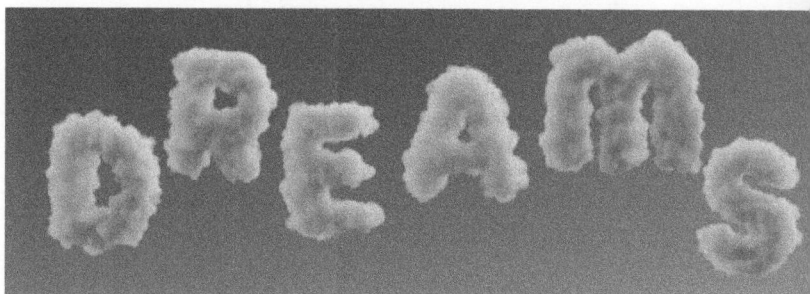

They first appear in whispers.
  Soft but clear words, unspoken.
  A small spark of inspiration,
  Untamed and unsought power.
  They create a bridge between souls.
  Heal wounds and make whole.
  Their magic is ink and air.
  Shaping hearts in the wisdom-growing regions.
  Words can be both cutting and healing.
  A powerful weapon, a balm that you can feel.
  The storm is calmed by lifting the broken.
  They are a force without form, but they can transform.
  We tell stories and sing songs.
  The truth is carried on fragile wings.
  Every letter and every line.
  The intertwined universe of dreams.
  The pen can become a powerful sword.
  The voice is a timeless and treasured chord.
  Words can break, but they can also mend.
  They are the ones who make the world turn.
  Use them with care and let them fly.

For words can open every door.
Let them ignite and discover their power
A beacon of hope and a world of optimism

ONE LAST THING

Thank you for selecting my book. I genuinely hope it has offered you an enjoyable and stimulating experience. I would appreciate your feedback and would be grateful if you could write a review on the platform where you bought it or on a book review site. Your feedback will help others make choices and show me which parts of the book were effective or lacking. Your honest review will help me grow as a writer and motivate me to create more engaging stories in the future.

Thank you once again for taking the time to explore my book. I genuinely hope it proved to be a rewarding experience for you. Your support means everything to me, and I am truly grateful to each reader who joins me on this journey. Together, we can cultivate a vibrant community of readers and writers united by our love for storytelling.

Each review contributes to a vibrant dialogue that enriches our literary experience. I look forward to hearing your thoughts and insights as we continue to explore the depths of creativity together. Your feedback is invaluable, and it inspires me to keep pushing the boundaries of my writing. Let's keep the conversation going and delve deeper into the stories that connect us all.

Book Haven
Scan the QR code for more information

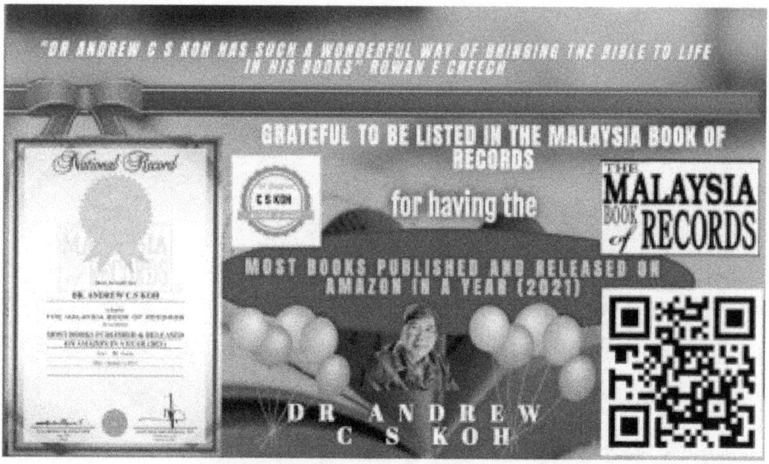

Scan The QR code to get a free book

Book Haven
Scan the QR code for more information

Scan the QR Code to get a free book

Don't miss out!

Visit the website below and you can sign up to receive emails whenever Dr Andrew C S Koh publishes a new book. There's no charge and no obligation.

https://books2read.com/r/B-A-FMXV-YROJF

BOOKS 2 READ

Connecting independent readers to independent writers.

Did you love *Mapping the Heart: The Doctor's Odyssey*? Then you should read *From Stethoscope to Wisdom: Reflection of a Doctor*[1] by Dr Andrew C S Koh!

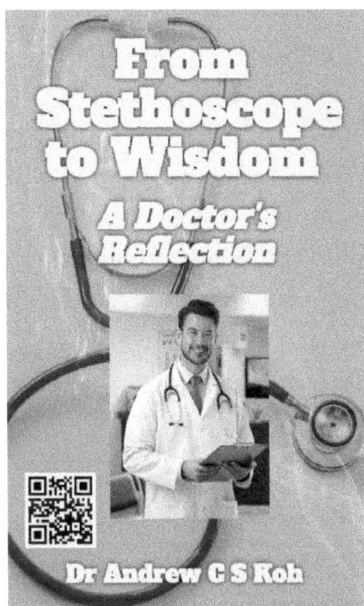

Readers are taken on an enlightening journey that explores the highs and lows of medical practice, laden with profound wisdom and heart-trending stories. This captivating memoir provides a rare, behind-the-scenes look at the life of a doctor, offering an earnest perspective on a profession often wrapped in mystery. Dr. Koh brings forth the realities of a sector where continuous learning, high pressure, critical decisions, and unpredictability are a part of everyday life. This book serves not just as an exploration of Dr. Koh's career in medicine but also sheds light on how this demanding career has shaped his understanding of life, suffering, recovery, and mortality. This book touches upon Dr. Koh's personal experiences throughout his remarkable journey across different hospitals, departments, and, ultimately, unique patient cases. It outlines the challenges faced, the victories enjoyed, and the lessons learned throughout his illustrious medical career. Dr. Andrew C.S Koh's book is not just a compelling read for those interested in the medical field. Its focus on empathy, strength, resilience, humility, and the power of the human spirit makes it a compelling read for all. This memoir embodies several life lessons that we all can draw from, regardless of our chosen profession. Readers will find this book to be more than just a recounting of a doctor's life. It is an invitation for us to appreciate the fragility and beauty of life, the resilience of the human spirit, and the immense courage and dedication hidden behind every medical professional's coat.

Read more at https://www.drandrewcskoh.com.

Also by Dr Andrew C S Koh

Daily Devotion
Manna of Life: Daily Devotion

Daily Devotions
Bread of Life Daily Devotions
Words of Eternal Life
Bread From Heaven: Daily Devotions
Light of the World Daily Devotions
Light of the World Daily Devotions
The Way, the Truth, and the Life

Genesis
Understanding Genesis 1-11: From Adam to Abraham
Faith Journey of Abraham: Genesis 12-25
Life Story of Jacob: Genesis 26-36
The Story of Joseph: Genesis 37-50

Gospels and Act

The Gospel According to Matthew
Daily Devotion Gospel of Mark
The Gospel According to Luke
Daily Devotion Gospel of John
Acts: Volume 1 and 2, From Jerusalem to Rome

Non Pauline and General Epistles
Hebrews: the Just Shall Live by Faith
1 John, 2 John, 3 John & Jude: a Verse by Verse Bible Study
General Epistles: 1 Peter, 2 Peter, James

Pauline Epistles
Romans: The Just Shall Live by Faith
1 Corinthians: The Greatest of These is Love
2 Corinthians: My Grace is Sufficient for You
1 Thessalonians, 2 Thessalonians, Philemon
Pastoral Epistles: 1 Timothy, 2 Timothy, Titus
Galatians: Justified by Faith in Jesus Christ
Philemon: Charge to the Master's Account

Prison Epistles
The Prison Epistles
Philippians: Rejoice Always in the Lord
Colossians: He is the Image of the Invisible God
Ephesians: Every Spiritual Blessing in the Heavenly Places in Christ

Watch for more at https://www.drandrewcskoh.com.

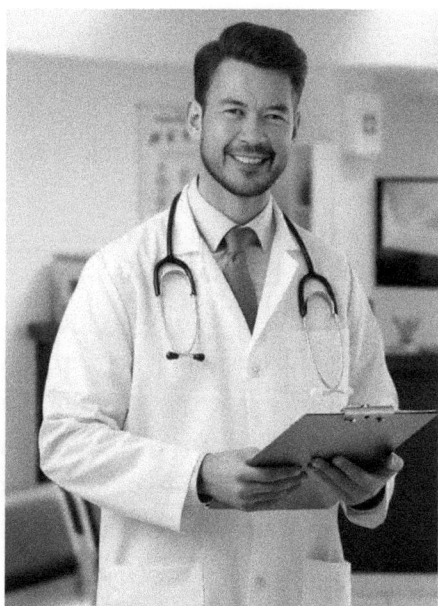

About the Author

Dr. Andrew C. S. Koh is a Christian author who has published 36 books. Beyond his role as an author, he is also a blogger, podcaster, bible teacher, digital creator, and retired cardiologist. He pursued theology at Laidlaw College in Auckland, New Zealand in 1999. Currently residing in Malaysia with his family, he finds joy in coffee, travel, and photography. He is listed in the Malaysia Book of Records for having the Most Books Published and Released in 2021.

Find out more about Andrew on:
https://linktr.ee/andrewcskoh
Search Andrew's books on:
https://books2read.com/ap/xX066D/Dr-Andrew-C-S-Koh
Get your free books on:
https://storyoriginapp.com/giveaways/b295be58-7736-11ec-ac4b-e34d930c508e
https://books2read.com/u/3kYJlN
Read more at https://www.drandrewcskoh.com.

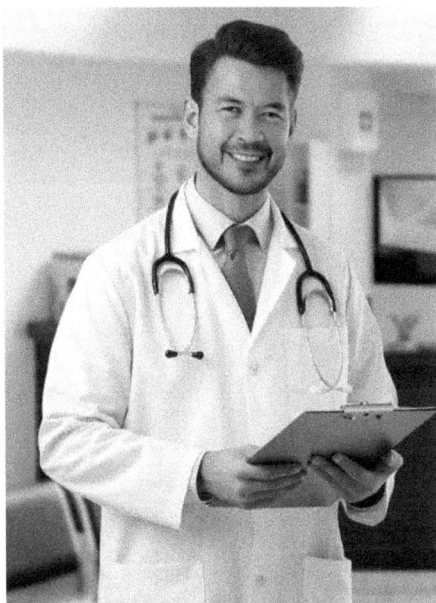

About the Publisher

Dr. Andrew C. S. Koh, a bestselling Amazon author, has authored 36 Christian books covering the New Testament, Old Testament, Bible study guides, and devotionals. Beyond his role as an author, he is a blogger, podcaster, bible teacher, and cardiologist. He pursued theology at Laidlaw College in Auckland, New Zealand in 1999.. Currently residing in Malaysia with his family, he finds joy in coffee, travel, and photography. He is listed in the Malaysia Book of Records for having the Most Books Published and Released in 2021.

Author of Memoirs of a Doctor:
https://dl.bookfunnel.com/hm2npovxom
Link Tree:
https://linktr.ee/andrewcskoh
Universal book link:
https://books2read.com/ap/xX066D/Dr-Andrew-C-S-Koh
New Release Notification:

https://books2read.com/author/dr-andrew-c-s-koh/subscribe/1/384961/

Free Books:

https://storyoriginapp.com/giveaways/b295be58-7736-11ec-ac4b-e34d930c508e

https://books2read.com/u/3kYJlN

Read more at https://www.drandrewcskoh.com.

www.ingramcontent.com/pod-product-compliance
Ingram Content Group UK Ltd.
Pitfield, Milton Keynes, MK11 3LW, UK
UKHW042047131224
452457UK00001B/55